THE GEOGRAPHERS' GUILD
LONDON
OF GREAT BRITAIN

PADDINGTON™ 2

Dear Aunt Lucy

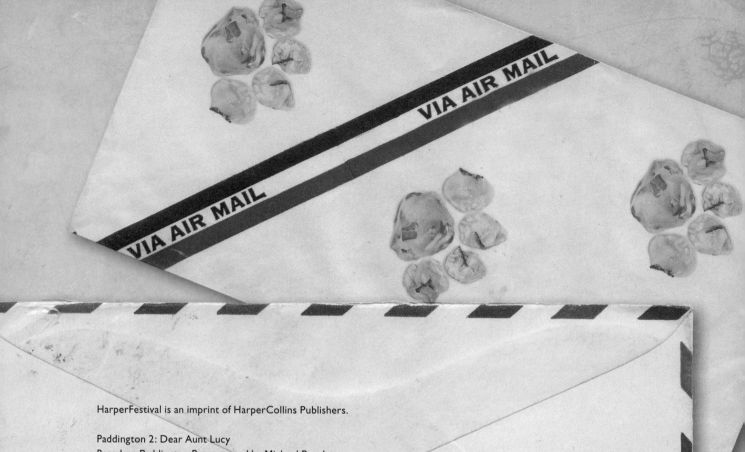

HarperFestival is an imprint of HarperCollins Publishers.

Paddington 2: Dear Aunt Lucy
Based on Paddington Bear created by Michael Bond
Paddington Bear™, Paddington™ and PB™ are trademarks of Paddington and Company Limited. Licensed on behalf of Studiocanal S.A.S. by Copyrights Group
www.harpercollinschildrens.com
ISBN 978-0-06-282440-0
17 18 19 20 21 CWM 10 9 8 7 6 5 4 3 2 1
❖
First Edition

THE GEOGRAPHERS GUILD
LONDON
OF GREAT BRITAIN.

PADDINGTON™ 2
Dear Aunt Lucy

Adapted by Thomas Macri
Based on Paddington Bear created
by Michael Bond

HARPER FESTIVAL
An Imprint of HarperCollinsPublishers

Dear Aunt Lucy,

It's been a few months since I left you and Darkest Peru behind to start a new life here in London. I think of you often, but even more so at this time of year, knowing your birthday is very soon.

London is as wonderful as you said it would be. But I do miss the rainforests of Peru. You don't see nearly as many trees here. The streets are always busy and full of people. Even traveling down the road can be troublesome.

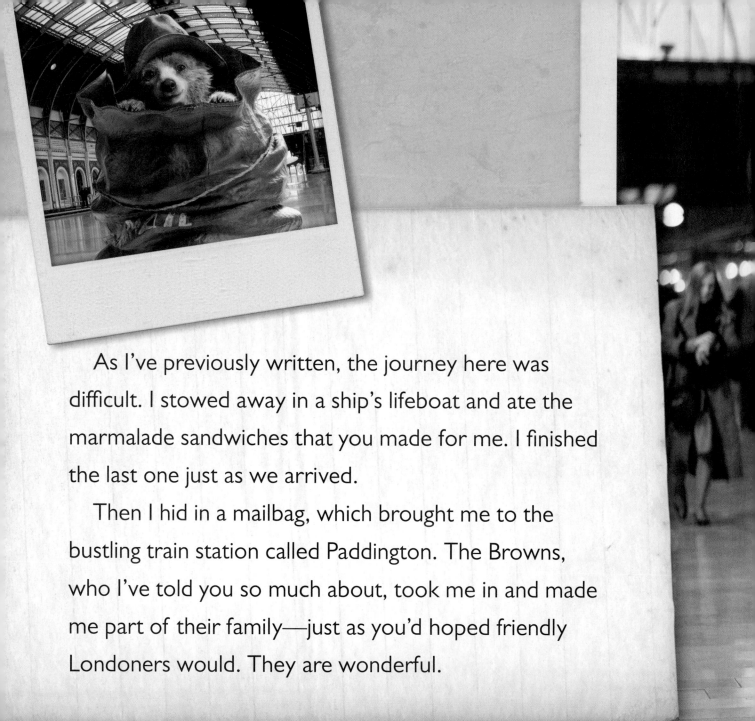

As I've previously written, the journey here was difficult. I stowed away in a ship's lifeboat and ate the marmalade sandwiches that you made for me. I finished the last one just as we arrived.

Then I hid in a mailbag, which brought me to the bustling train station called Paddington. The Browns, who I've told you so much about, took me in and made me part of their family—just as you'd hoped friendly Londoners would. They are wonderful.

As I've told you before, Mr. Brown is a funny sort of fellow. He can be very serious, but then lets loose at times. He's currently practicing a funny thing called yoga, which is something humans do to put their bodies in unnatural and terribly uncomfortable positions.

Mrs. Brown is a spectacular artist who is never short of wildly creative ideas. And she's sporty as well—she is currently training to swim the English Channel, which is not quite as wide as the Pacific Ocean, but far broader than the Ucayali River back home.

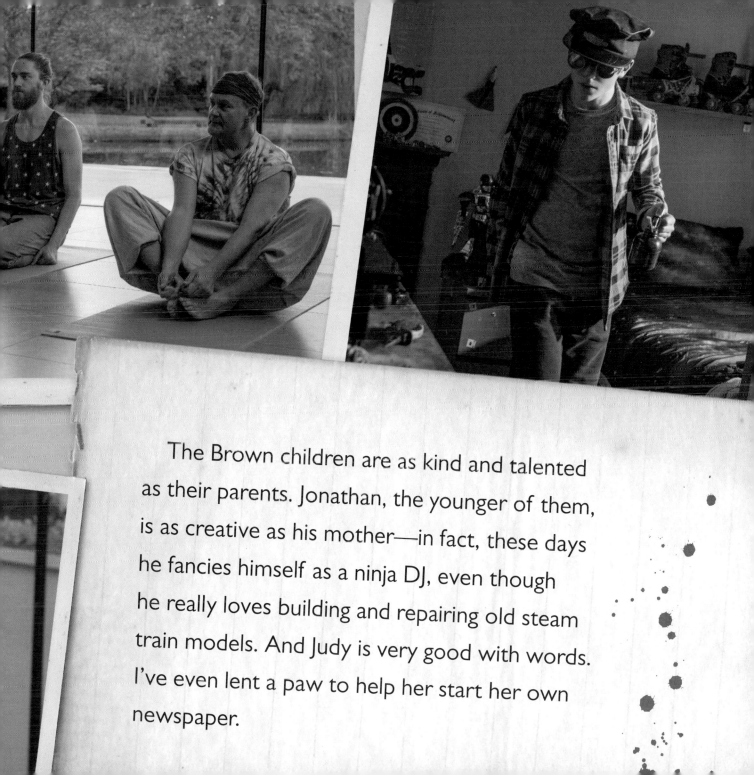

The Brown children are as kind and talented as their parents. Jonathan, the younger of them, is as creative as his mother—in fact, these days he fancies himself as a ninja DJ, even though he really loves building and repairing old steam train models. And Judy is very good with words. I've even lent a paw to help her start her own newspaper.

Sadly, not everyone in London is as nice as the Browns. Mr. Curry, their next-door neighbor, is always acting oddly toward me. He is a very suspicious fellow and is always convinced I've done something wrong.

THE GEOGRAPHERS' GUILD
LONDON
OF GREAT BRITAIN

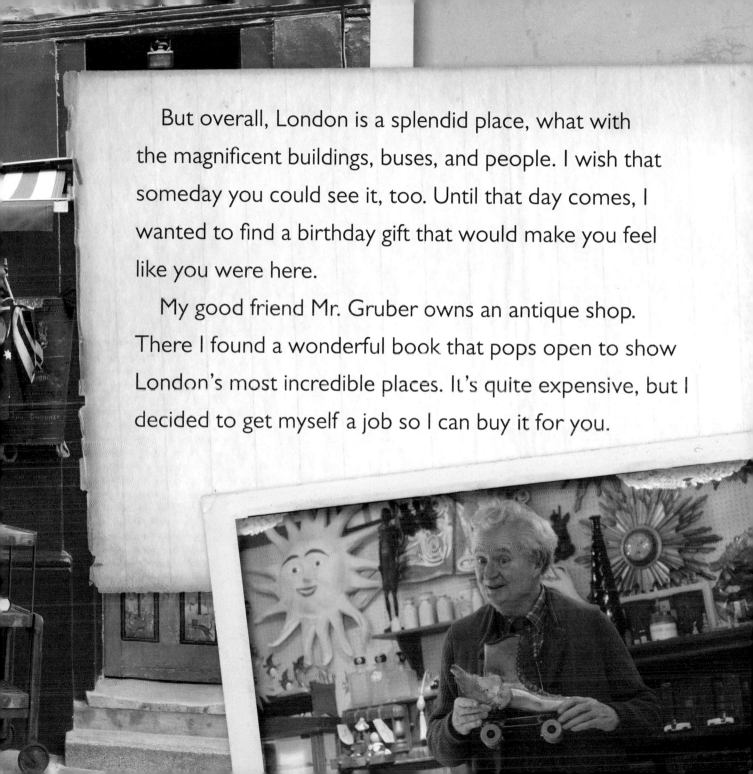

But overall, London is a splendid place, what with the magnificent buildings, buses, and people. I wish that someday you could see it, too. Until that day comes, I wanted to find a birthday gift that would make you feel like you were here.

My good friend Mr. Gruber owns an antique shop. There I found a wonderful book that pops open to show London's most incredible places. It's quite expensive, but I decided to get myself a job so I can buy it for you.

I worked very hard to earn the money. I never turned down an opportunity to take an odd job wherever I could find one. I did everything from washing windows to cutting hair. I was very good at washing windows.

I can hardly wait to purchase the book. Mr. Gruber thinks it's the perfect gift.

Curiously, our new neighbor, Phoenix Buchanan, seems excited about the book, too. Mr. Buchanan is an actor who was invited to open Madame Kozlova's World-Famous Steam Fair. He used to be famous but has since fallen out of favor, and the only film work he does now is dog food commercials.

Phoenix is hoping to open his own show in London's West End, where many of the best actors perform. He is charming and talented, and the entire Brown family is excited to see his act. He lives in the same street as the Browns.

Phoenix always asks me a lot of questions about the book. After all, it is so beautiful. Turning the pages makes you feel as though you're really in this great city.

I do wish you could be here to see the real thing.

I often imagine what it would be like for us to be together again.

One day, I certainly hope we will be.

With love from

Padingtun